the MARVELLOUS
FLUFFY
SQUISHY ITTY BITTY

'Children need a little order in their lives.
Especially when they can order it themselves!'
PIPPI LONGSTOCKING

Many thanks to Paola, Béatrice, Olivier,
Emmanuel, William and Alix – B.A.

Translated from the French *Le merveilleux dodu-velu-petit*

First published in the United Kingdom in 2015 by
Thames & Hudson Ltd, 181A High Holborn, London WC1V 7QX

This paperback edition first published in 2019

British Library Cataloguing-in-Publication Data
A catalogue record for this book is available from the British Library

ISBN 978-0-500-65193-3

Printed in China

To find out about all our publications, please visit
www.thamesandhudson.com. There you can subscribe
to our e-newsletter, browse or download our current
catalogue, and buy any titles that are in print.

BEATRICE ALEMAGNA

the MARVELLOUS FLUFFY SQUISHY ITTY BITTY

Thames & Hudson

My name is Edith, but my
friends call me Eddie.
I'm five and a half years old.

My dad speaks five languages,
my mum has a lovely singing voice,
my sister is a brilliant ice-skater,
but I'm not very good at anything.

Nothing much at all.
Or at least, that's what I used to think.

One morning, I heard my sister saying the words 'present... Mum... birthday... fluffy... squishy... itty... bitty...'

Oh dear, I thought. She was going to buy an amazing present for Mum. Now I should get her a present too. But what should I get?

Quick, off to Bruno's bakery!
He sells all sorts of delicious things.
I bet he can help me.

'Hi Bruno! Do you have a Fluffy Squishy
Itty Bitty for sale?'

'A fishy squidgy what? Sorry, Eddie.
That doesn't sound very tasty,' said Bruno.
'But I do have some lovely warm sticky buns.
Would you like one to take with you?'

With the bun in my bag, I went to visit Wendy,
who has the prettiest flower shop in town.

'A furry squirty what?' said Wendy.
'That sounds like a very strange plant indeed.
But here's a four-leaf clover.
Take it with you, it might bring you luck!'

Mimi's fashion shop was full of furry, feathery things.
Surely I would find a Fluffy Squishy Itty Bitty there?

'A frilly swishy what?' said Mimi.
'That doesn't sound very stylish to me.
Here, take this instead. It's much prettier!'

It was a pearl button. My search wasn't going very well. So I decided to go and see the most stylish person I know.

My friend Emmett
at the antique shop!

'A floppy squashy what?' said Emmett.
'Sorry Eddie, there's nothing like that in here.
But here's something much better.
A Threepenny Green! It's a very rare stamp.
I'm sure your mum will love it.'

An old stamp? I wasn't having much luck.

I wandered down the street but nobody knew where I could find a Fluffy Squishy Itty Bitty. In the town square, I saw Theo in his butcher's shop. He was my last hope.

'A flabby squeaky what?' yelled Theo, pointing his big nasty finger at me. 'I'm far too busy to answer your silly questions today. Go away and bother somebody else!'

Eeek! I was so scared that I ran away as fast as my legs could carry me.

Then it started to snow.
Feeling cold and sad, I looked for somewhere to shelter.

Then I heard a noise from up on the roof.
It sounded like giggling. I couldn't believe it,
but there it was.

What an adorable creature! Not very tasty,
not very stylish, but fluffy, squishy, strange
and rare. It was a real Fluffy Squishy Itty Bitty,
the perfect present and useful for so many things!

Using the sticky bun that Bruno had given me,
I tried to lure the Fluffy Squishy Itty Bitty
down from the roof. But suddenly
it slipped and...

...CRASH! It dropped into a dustbin, just as Quentin the dustman was collecting the rubbish. I begged him to open it. 'Don't be silly,' said Quentin. 'I'm not opening a bin for a bit of old rag.'

What I needed was good luck. I reached into my pocket to touch Wendy's four-leaf clover and Emmett's old stamp fell on the ground.

Suddenly Quentin turned around.

'Hey, what's that?' asked Quentin.
'It's a Threepenny Green,' I said. 'It's very rare.'
'Wow, I don't have one of those in my stamp
collection,' he said. 'Will you sell it to me?'
'I won't sell it, but I will swap it for what's in that
bin!' I said.

Yuck! The Fluffy Squishy Itty Bitty had
rolled around in the bin and now it was all
smelly. I could give it a bath, but where?
There was a fountain in the square but I'd
need a coin to switch it on.

But there was no money in my pockets,
just the pearl button that Mimi gave me.
Well, it was worth a try. I put the button in
the slot and waited...

A few seconds later, the fountain began to spin.
Beautiful jets of water sprayed out all around.
It was just like magic! Everyone clapped their
hands and I gave the Fluffy Squishy Itty Bitty
a good wash.

What a day it had been. I'd done something that nobody else had done before. And I'd finally found out what I was good at. I was the best Fluffy Squishy Itty Bitty finder in the world.

Back at home, Mum was delighted.
'What a marvellous present! It's fluffy, it's squishy
and it's itty bitty! Was it you who found this?'

'Yes, Mum!' I said. 'With a little help from
my marvellous friends.'

The End